CRYPTOMANIA!

Teleporting into Greek and Latin with the CryptoKids

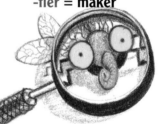
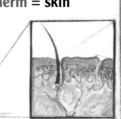

STELLA

Greetings! Stella means "star" in Latin. Come with us on a stellar adventure!

Zander here. My friends and I are the CryptoKids. We're ready for adventure!

ZANDER

What's up? Zander's short for Alexander, as in Alexander the Great.

Hey there! Theo's short for Theodore, a Greek name. I can't wait to see what Zander's up to.

THEO

helicopter
helico = spiral
pter = wing

dinosaur
dino = terrible
saur, saurus = lizard

Microcyanosaurus
micro- = small
cyano- = blue
saur, saurus = lizard

Call me Alphy!

acrobat
acro- = high
bat = step, go

triangle
tri- = three
angul = angle

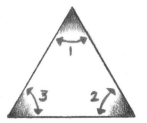

tripod
tri- = three
pod = foot

CryptoKid

crypto = hidden, secret
kid = young person who hunts for answers—

You!

To all the real CryptoKids at Park Dale Lane Elementary School.
You're simply stellar! —EHF

To Richard Peck, Mona Meisami, Betsy Perry, and especially Catherine Jacobes:
gratias tibi ago. To brilliant author Edith Hope Fine: kudos, magnum kudos. This
book is for Nicole Geiger—editor extraordinaire, visionary, mentor. Vivat! —KD

ACKNOWLEDGMENTS
Believe me, to build this book for all you CryptoKids to dig into takes
teamwork. My thanks to: Nicole Geiger, editor; Catherine Jacobes, designer;
Kim Doner, illustrator; Vincent McCarren, Ph.D., language consultant; Nancy
Champlin and Suzan Wilson, teachers; Wade Fox, copy editor; Sharon Silva and
Jasmine Star, proofreaders; and intuitive family and friends. —Edith Hope Fine

Tricycle Press
a little division of Ten Speed Press
P.O. Box 7123
Berkeley, California 94707
www.tenspeed.com

Book design by Catherine Jacobes Design

Library of Congress Cataloging-in-Publication Data

Fine, Edith Hope.
  Cryptomania!: teleporting into Greek and Latin with the CryptoKids /
by Edith Hope Fine ; illustrations by Kim Doner.
     p. cm.
Summary: A group of friends teleports to worlds of Greek and Latin words
while trying to complete a vocabulary assignment in time to celebrate
their town's centennial.
  ISBN 1-58246-062-0
  [1. Space and time—Fiction. 2. English language—Etymology. 3. Greek
language. 4. Latin language.] I. Doner, Kim, 1955– ill. II. Title.
PZ7.F495674 Cr 2003
[Fic]—dc21
                                        2002155805

First printing, 2004

Printed in China
1 2 3 4 5 6 — 08 07 06 05 04

iv

CRYPTOMANIA!

by **EDITH HOPE FINE**

Illustrated by **KIM DONER**

Tricycle Press
Berkeley | Toronto

CONTENTS

Calling All CryptoKids

Figuring out big English words like aqueous, hydroelectric, zoology, and pachyderm can be a snap. All you need are clues from the past.

Long ago, many people spoke Greek or Latin every day. There are still people today who speak Greek, and some religious ceremonies still use Latin. Knowing a little Greek and Latin is like wearing a secret decoder's cape—you can work out the meanings of many English words you've never even seen before—**big** words, **hard** words.

When you know chunks of Greek and Latin, you can . . .
- figure out words you didn't think you knew!
- learn faster and easier!
- astound your friends and family!

And here's the great part. You probably already know some Greek and Latin.

Aqua and hydr or hydro- mean "water" —think of aquariums and fire hydrants. Now if you come across big words like "aqueous" and "hydroelectric," you can make a smart guess that they have something to do with water—and you'll be right.

Tri- means "three." A triple ice cream cone has three scoops. A triangle has three angles.

Cent- means "hundred." A century is 100 years.

Zo- means "animal." You see animals at the zoo. And if you become a zoologist, you'll study animals.

Pachy means "thick" and derm means "skin." No wonder rhinos, hippos, and elephants are called "pachyderms" (say, "PACK-ih-derms")— they have thick hides.

Join Alphy and the CryptoKids as they teleport through time and space. Help solve a mystery, discover some keys, and unlock a few new worlds for yourself!

English has more than 600,000 words! More than half of these come from Greek and Latin.

Decoding Secret
Latin word parts are red.
Greek word parts are green.

Roots, Prefixes, Suffixes

Roots are main word parts. The roots thermo- and therm- mean "heat." Think of a thermometer or thermal underwear.

Prefixes go before roots. The prefix sub- means "under." Think of subway, submarine.

Suffixes go after roots. The suffix -ify means "to make." Think of petrify— to make into stone (petr-).

pre- = before
suf- = directly after
fixus = fastened, fixed

Cross your toes, Blue Dino. If we can teleport you home, maybe we can teleport ourselves past the homework due Friday, too. That'd sure be my key to a fun Centennial.

When you figure out a tough word, shout, "Eureka!" That's Greek for "I have found [it]!" Saying "Eureka" shows your excitement when you discover something new.

IN PROCESS
logo = word
scop = look at
stetho = chest
tri- = three
ped, pod = foot
-al = of, relating to
ortho- = straight
odon, odont = tooth
-ist = an expert in
cardio- = heart
vascul = tube, vessel
-ar = relating to
-graph, -gram = write, draw
photo- = light
Ta-da! I just invented a word machine—a Logoscope. Drop Greek and Latin word chunks in here; they hook up so that big words come out there! This may help us with our vocab homework.
How neat! And I'll post photos from our Greek and Roman adventure. "Photograph" means "drawn with light."
Logoscope
stethoscope
tripod
podium
pedal
orthodontist
cardiovascular system
cardiogram
photograph
Well, the light sure drew some funny colors. I wonder what's happening.
Speaking of what's happening, we'd better find out where we're going next. We still need to take Alphy home. Let's turn this key to find keys to new worlds.
bi- = two
lingu = tongue, language
If you're bilingual, like Alphy, you can speak two languages.
That key will turn easier than the keystone I saw on the Roman aqueduct. Here comes the clue! "You left off the 'pre' and got Greece and Rome. Be way more specific to get Alphy home."
Vale, Roma atque Graecia! Farewell, Rome and Greece!
What's purple and conquered the world?
Alexander the Grape.
To speak like a Roman, say, "WAH-lay ROH-mah AHT-kweh GREH-kee-ah."
Wow! Traveling through time and space is great! And we made it back to the Teleporter okay.

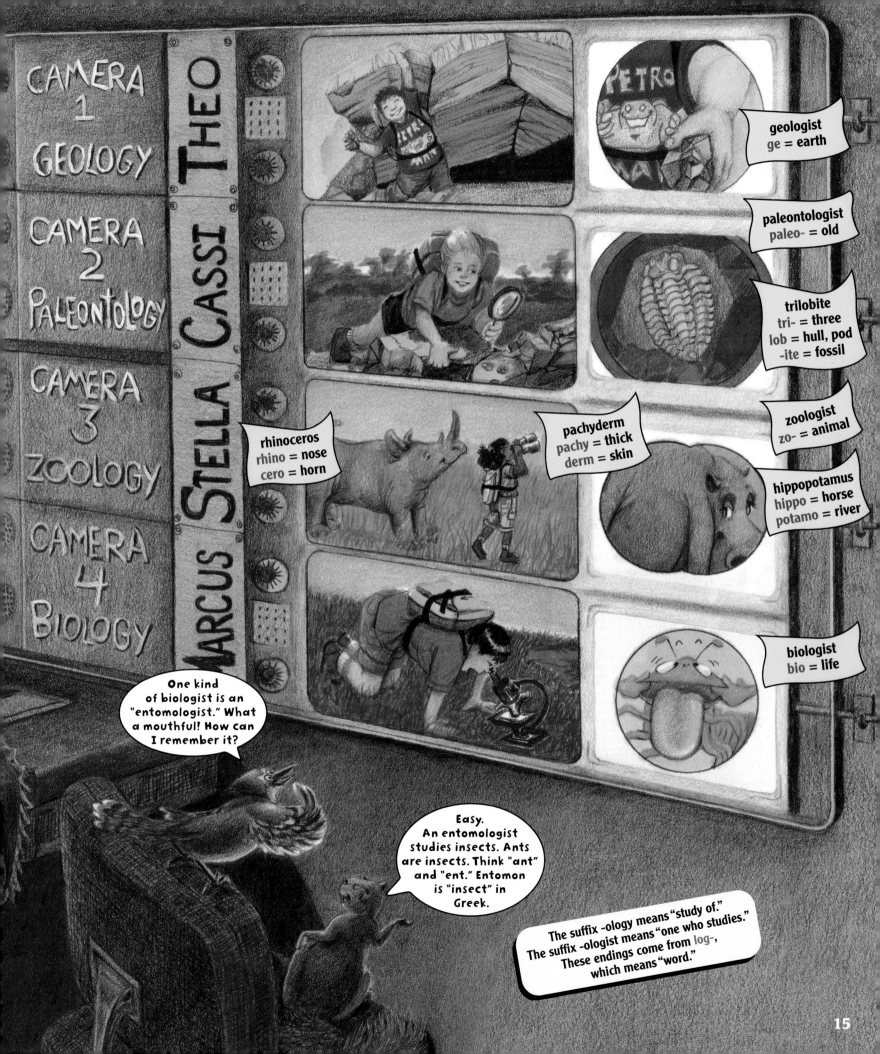

15

IN PROCESS

litho-, petr-, petro- = rock, stone
-ify = to make
glyph = carving
-phyt = plant
bi-, bin- = two
ocul = eye
micro- = small
scop = look at
ge = earth
-ology = study of
-graphy = writing
bio = life
photo- = light
trop = turn, change
atmo = vapor
sphere (sphaîra) = globe, sphere

The atmosphere is the air that surrounds Earth. Gravity holds the five gassy layers of the atmosphere in place.

This calm, spread-out layer includes the ozone layer. It helps protect Earth from ultraviolet rays.

Closest to Earth, this layer is wild, windy, churny, turny. Think "tropics"—fast-changing weather!

The mesosphere's easy. It's the middle layer.

EARTH & ITS ATMOSPHERE

troposphere   trop = turn, change

stratosphere   strat- = spread out

mesosphere   meso- = middle

ionosphere
ion = go
(say, "EYE-on")

exosphere   exo- = outer

This layer gives me a charge! An ion is an atom with a positive or a negative electrical charge.

The exosphere is far out! It's Earth's outer layer of air. Hey, Alphy, what's our next clue?

"You'd better take a different route. Think 'gigabytes.' Go on! Reboot!"

petrify
petroglyph
lithophyte
binoculars
microscope
geology
geography
biology
phototropic
atmosphere

Alphy's teacher taught him the five layers of Earth's atmosphere in five minutes. I'll bet we can top that!

The smallest piece of information a computer can understand is called a bit—that's short for **bi**nary digit. Bits are "on" and "off" electric signals, and are shown with a zero (for off) or a one (for on). Since these are only two numbers, computer languages are **bi**nary.

It's a pattern! So if a light is on, it's a "one" and you count that place value. If it's off, it's a "zero." Don't count it. Here, I see that only the ones place and the fours place lights are on. And four plus one is five. One-zero-one shows five in binary.

Eight bits make a byte (say, "bite"). A byte makes one letter or one number.

If we could see bits, this is how they'd stack up next to bytes.

one bit

one byte

Place value is different, too. The decimal system has the ones place, the tens, the hundreds, and so on. The binary system has the ones place, the twos, the fours, the eights... get it?

magnifier
magn- = large
-fier = maker

BINARY SYSTEM PLACE VALUES

SIXTEENS	EIGHTS	FOURS	TWOS	ONES
0	0	1	0	1
16	8	4	2	1

A binary 5 looks like 101.

Did you know that cursor is Latin for "runner"?

And deletus is Latin for "destroyed" or "erased." Delete—get it?

21

Surf 'n' Sky

stella, aster, astro- = star
naut = sailor
uni- = one
versus = turn (into)

con- = together   stella = star
-tion = state of, condition
Constellations are groups of stars
that form shapes, like animals or
mythological characters.

The Big and Little Dippers are asterisms—
not official constellations but groups of
stars that are easy to spot. The Big Dipper
is in the constellation Ursa Major.
The Little Dipper is in Ursa Minor.

I want to
be an astronaut.
I'll sail the stars
and explore the
universe.

I know
a lot of constellations.
See how the edge of the
Big Dipper points to
Polaris, the North
Star?

Whoa!
There it is!

Finally, we get to relax. Our homework
and the Centennial can wait.

25

MATHOPOLIS

Home of the Famous Flats! This Week:
The Mathopolis Flats vs. The Hedronville 3-Ds

mathema = knowledge, learning

polis = city

poly- = many gon = angle
hedr = side
Polygons are closed, flat figures made up of three or more line segments. Polyhedrons are 3-D and have polygons for sides.

Sidney Square

Trixie Triangle

Rufus Rectangle

The Polygons

Carla Cube

Perry Pyramid

Rupert Rectangular Prism

The Polyhedrons

Sam Sphere

Cyrus Circle

This place is just plain weird!

parallelos = beside one another
Parallel lines never meet.
A parallelogram has four sides.
The top and bottom are parallel.
The two sides are parallel.

Ah, Mathopolis, where everything adds up.

I'm a centipede. I may not have a hundred feet, but I have a lot!

MATHOPOLIS DAILY

Today's Riddles:
What geometrical shape is like a lost parrot?

What did the math teacher serve for snacks?

Answer Key
A polygon.
Gram crackers!

Well, I'm a millipede. And I don't really have a thousand feet, but I have more than that guy!

centi- = 100
mill- = 1,000
ped = foot

noven-

dec-
decem-
dec-
deca-

tri-
tri-

quin-
penta-

sept-
hepta-

sex-
hex-

oct-
octo-

quad-
tetra-

bi-
di-

uni-
mono-

26

27

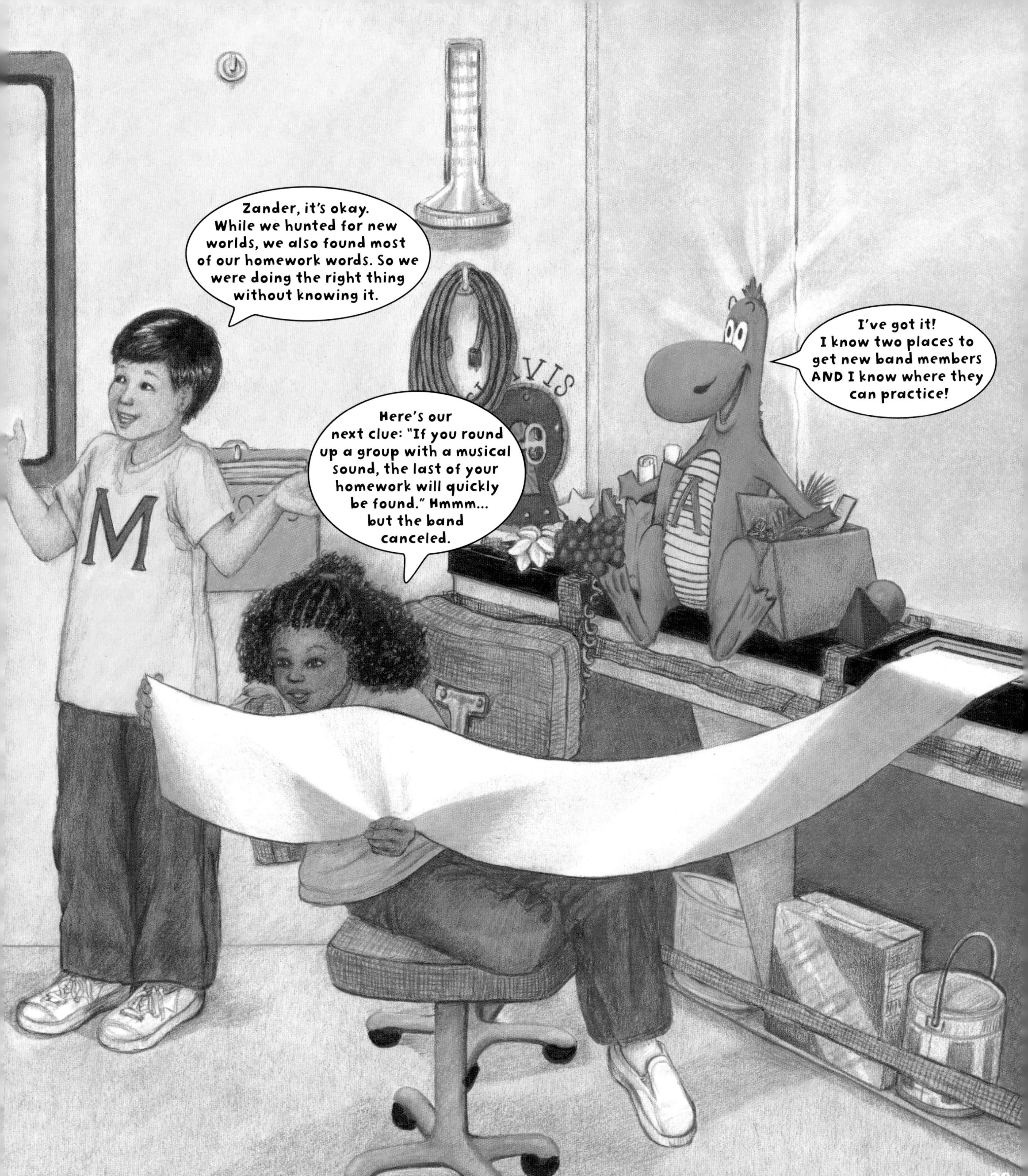
Zander, it's okay. While we hunted for new worlds, we also found most of our homework words. So we were doing the right thing without knowing it.
Here's our next clue: "If you round up a group with a musical sound, the last of your homework will quickly be found." Hmmm... but the band canceled.
I've got it! I know two places to get new band members AND I know where they can practice!

Polyphonic

poly- = many
son, phon = sound
-ic = of, relating to

calliope (say, "kah-LIE-uh-pea")
calli = beautiful ops = voice
In Greek mythology, Calliope was the muse of heroic tales, like Homer's "Iliad" and "Odyssey."

auto- = self
An autoharp automatically plays a chord when you press one or more buttons and strum the strings.

Tuba is a real Latin word! The Roman tuba was a type of trumpet.

This is the best band of all—a band of friends.

The band sounds good already.

Wow! Unexpectedly excellent! Alphy saved the day with his super-phonic-sonic idea.

audit = hear
-orium = place for

STAR LAKE AUDITORIUM

NOTICE:
ONE DAY LEFT for Centennial booth entries
Tempus fugit!
Time flies!

Such euphonious music!

Yup—nothing phony about it.

To Mathopolis and Alphasaurus Academy and back. That was a lot of teleporting, but we made it just in time.

eu- = good
phon = sound
-ious = having

Philharmonic

clavichord
clavis = key
chorda = string

cymbalum, kymbalon = cymbal

phil = love of
harmon- = harmony
-ic = of, relating to

triangle
tri- = three
angul = angle

POLYPHONIC PHILHARMONIC

PERCUSSION SECTION

And phil means "love of," like somebody crazy about books is a "bibliophile." I'll bet harmonic is like "harmony"—you know, like many notes that go together. We've done it—the Mega-Word Opus! Finished!

Well, poly means "many"—we got that in Mathopolis. Phon means "sound." Polyphonic—making many sounds? Or sounds working together?

Polyphonic Philharmonic? I can't believe it! Those are our last two vocab words. Let's figure them out.

xylophone
xylo- = wood
phon = sound

The Roman Alphabet
Many Latin words come from ancient Greek language roots. The Romans used 23 capital letters for writing Latin: A B C D E F G H I K L M N O P Q R S T V X Y Z. Romans only used the K X Y and Z for writing words that came from Greek. The K of Greek is changed to C in Latin and English.

Greek & Latin Glossary & Index

-phon ii, 31, 32, phono- 32, phon 30, 31, 32 = sound
photo- ii, 8, 16 = light
-phyt 16 = plant
planetes 23 = planet, wanderer
planum 25 = flat surface, plane
pod iii, 6, 8, 11, 21, 35 = foot
Polaris 23 = North Star, polestar
polis 26 = city
poly- 11, 26, 28, 30, 35 = many
port 2 = bear, carry
post- 6 = after
posterior 7 = bottom
potamo 15 = river
pous 6, 21 = foot
pre- 2, 4, 5, 7, 8 = before
pter iii, ptero 10, 35 = wing
pulmon 7 = lung

quaenam 23 = how
quest- 21 = search
radius 27 = beam of light, staff
re- 17, 20 = again
rex 10 = king
rhino- 6, 12, 15, 35 = nose
Roma 8 = Rome
saur iii, 10, 12, 35, saurus iii, 10, 12 = lizard
scop ii, 2, 8, 16, 23, 24 = examine, look at
scrib 1, 36, script 36 = record, write, written
skeleto 21 = skeleton
sol 24, 36 = sun
son 30, 32 = sound
sphere (sphaîra) 13, 16 = globe, sphere
stella 10, 22, 23, 24 = star
stetho 6, 8 = chest
strat- 16 = spread out
sub- 4, 24 = under

suf- 4 = directly after
super- 32 = above, over
sym- 32 = together, with
tele- 2, 23, 24, 32 = distant, far
terra 13 = earth
therm- 4, thermo- 4, 10, 12 = heat
thesauros 11 = treasury
trop 16 = change, turn
tuba 30 = tuba
tyranno 10 = tyrant
umbr- 21 = shade
ursa 23 = bear (animal)
vale 8 = farewell (good-bye)
vascul 8 = tube, vessel
versus 22 = turn (into)
virus 20 = poison
xylo- 31 = wood
zo- 4, 10, 12, 15 = animal

English Glossary & Index

about = circa 6
above, over = super- 32
across = dia- 27
after = post- 6
again = re- 17, 20
and = atque 8
and a half = sesqui- 27
angle = angul iii, 11, 28, 31, gon 26, 27, 28
animal = zo- 4, 10, 12, 15
around = circum-, peri- 28, 36
back, backward = ana- 6
beam of light = radius 27
bear (animal) = ursa 23
bear (carry) = fer 28, port 2
beautiful = bella 23, calli 30, 37, kal ii
before = pre- 2, 4, 5, 6, 8
beside one another, parallel = parallelos 26
between = inter- 17
big, great, large, = magn- ii, 19, mega- ii, 2, 6, 13, 20, 31, 35, 36
blue = cyano- iii, 2, 10, 35
blue jay = Cyanocitta 2
book = libr- 35, biblio- 11
bottom = posterior 7
carry, bear = fer 28, port 2
carving = glyph 16
center = centr- 24
change = meta- 12, trop 16
chest = stetho 6, 8
circle, wheel = cycl- 20
city = polis 26
clarify = illustra 1
clavicle = clavicula 7
color = chromo- 11, 35
composition, a work = opus 2, 6, 13, 31
convey, lead = duct 7

correct, straight = ortho- 8
count = comput- 18, 20
curiosity = curiositas 38
cymbal = cymbalum, kymbalon 31
destroyed, erased = deletus 19
device for measuring = -meter 10, 12
directly after = suf- 4
distant, far = tele- 2, 23, 24, 32
draw, record, write, written = -gram 8, -graph ii, 8, 32, 36
earth = terra 13, ge 15,16
endlessly, to infinity = ad infinitum 34
equal = equi- 28
erased, destroyed = deletus 19
examine, look at = scop ii, 2, 8, 16, 23, 24
external, outer, outside = exo- 16, 21
eye = ocul 7, 16, ops 6, 35, opt 6
face = ops 10, 11, 35
far, distant = tele- 2, 23, 24, 32
farewell (good-bye) = vale 8
fastened, fixed = fixus 4
finger, toe = digit 7, dactyl 6, 10, 35
firm, solid = firma 13
flat surface, plane = planum 25
foot = ped 7, 8, 26, 27, pous 6, 21, pod iii, 6, 8, 11, 21, 35
form, shape = eido- ii, morph 11, 12
gigantic, huge = giga 20
glitter, twinkle = mica 23
globe = glob 13, sphere (sphaîra) 13, 16
go = ion 16
go, step = bat- iii
going around = circuitus 18, 20
good = eu- 30
great, big, large = magn- ii, 19 mega- ii, 2, 6, 13, 20, 31, 35, 36

a great work, masterpiece = magnum opus 36
Greece = Graecia 8
hail (hello) = ave 7, 8
hand = manu 7
harmony = harmon- 31, 32
head = capit 7, cephal 6, cephalo 10, 11, 12, 21, 35
hear, hearing = audio 32, audit 30
heart = cardi 6, cardio- 8
heat = therm- 4, thermo- 4, 10, 12
hidden, secret = crypto iii, 1, 18
high = acro- iii
horn = cornu 12, cerat- 10, 11, 35, cero 12, 15
horse = hippo 15
how = quaenam 23
huge, gigantic = giga 20
hull, pod = lob 15
I have found [it]! = Eureka! 4, 39, 40
I wonder = miror 23
illuminate = illustra 1
imagining = imagin- 33
in = in- (also into), en- 18
information = informatio- 18
inner, inside, within = endo- 21
insect = entomon 15
island = insula 21
jay = kitta 2
keepsake = memento 24
key = clavis 1, 31
king = rex 10
knowledge, learning = mathema 26
large, big, great = magn- ii, 19, mega- ii, 2, 6, 13, 20, 31, 35, 36
language = lingua 8
law = nom ii, 24

lead, convey = duct 7
life = bio 15, 16
light = photo- ii, 8, 16
little, small = -ella 21, parva 23, micro- iii, 10, 16, 35
little key = clavicula 7
little star = asterisk 23
lizard = saur iii, 10, 12, 35, saurus iii, 10, 12
look at, examine = scop ii, 2, 8, 16, 23, 24
love of = phil 31, 32
lung = pulmon 7
machine = machina 18
make bright = illustra 1
maker = -fier ii, 19
major = maior 23
many = poly- 11, 26, 28, 30, 35
masterpiece, a great work = magnum opus 36
measure, a unit of measure = meter 27, 28
    device for measuring = -meter 10, 12, 32
memento, keepsake = memento
    (from the verb "to remember") 24
middle = meso- 10, 16
moon = luna 23
moving = mobile 5
my fault = mea culpa 7, 28, 36
new = ceno- 10
North Star (polestar) = Polaris 23
nose = rhino 6, 12, 15, 35
not, without = a- 11
number = numer 28, arithm 25, 28
old = paleo- 10, 15
on, upon = epi- ii
one who loves = -phile 11
one who studies = -ologist (from log-) 15
onomatopoeia = onomatopoeia 32
outer, outside, external = exo- 16, 21
over, above = super- 32
parallel, beside one another = parallelos 26
peace = pax 36
plane, flat surface = planum 25
planet, wanderer = planetes 23
plant = -phyt 16
plenty = copia 12
pod, hull = lob 15
poison = virus 20
polestar (North Star) = Polaris 23
record, write, written = scrib 1, 36 script 36, -gram 8, -graph (also draw) ii, 8, 32, 36
remember, keepsake = memento 24
river = potamo 15
rock, stone = litho- 14, 16, petr- 4, 16 petro- 14, 16
Rome = Roma 8
runner = cursor 19
sailor = naut 22, 24
sea = mar 24
search = quest- 21
secret, hidden = crypto iii, 1, 18

self = auto- 30
shade = umbr- 21
shake, strike = cuss 32
shape, form = eido- ii, morph 11, 12
ship = nau, nav, naut 24
side = later (LAH-ter) 28, hedr 26, 28
skeleton = skeleto 21
skin = derm ii, 4, 6, 15
small, little = -ella 21, parva 23, micro- iii, 10, 16, 35
solid, firm = firma 13
sound = son 30, 32, phon ii, 30, 31, 32, phono- 32
sphere = glob 13, sphere (sphaîra) 13, 16
spiral = helico iii
spread out = strat- 16
staff = radius 27
star = stella iii, 10, 22, 23, 24, aster 22, astro- 10, 22, 24
steer (verb) = cybern- 18, 20
step, go = bat iii
stone, rock = litho- 14, 16, petr- 4, 16, petro- 14, 16
straight, correct = ortho- 8
strike, shake = cuss 32
string = chorda 31
study of, science of = -ology (from log-) 15, 16
sun = sol, helio- 24, 36
terrible = dino iii, 10
thick = pachy 4, 10, 12, 15, 35
through = per- 32
time = chron 6, chrono- 5,
to infinity, endlessly = ad infinitum 34
toe, finger = digit 7, dactyl 6, 10, 35
together, with = con- 22, 24, sym- 32
tongue = lingu 8
tooth = dent 7, odon, odont 6, 8
treasury = thesauros 11
tuba = tuba 30
tube, vessel = vascul 8
turn = trop 16
turn (into) = versus 22,
twinkle, glitter = mica 23
tyrant = tyranno 10
under = sub- 4, 24
unit of measure = meter 28
universe = cosmo- 24
upon, on = epi- ii
vapor (gas) = atmo 16
vessel, tube = vascul 8
voice = ops 30, 35
wanderer, planet = planetes 23
water = aqua ii, 4, 7, 24, hydr- 4, 24 hydro- 4, 14
wheel, circle = cycl- 20
why = cur 38
wing = pter iii, ptero 10, 35
with, together = con- 22, 24, sym- 32

within, inner, inside = endo- 21
without, not = a- 11
wood = xylo 31
word = log- 15, logo 2, 8, 11
a work, composition = opus 2, 6, 13, 31
write, written, record = scrib 1, 36, script 36, -gram 8, -graph (also draw) ii, 8, 32, 36
writing = -graph 8, 32, 36, -graphy 16, 37
year = annu-, -enni, 2

Suffixes from Greek & Latin
These English suffixes have come from Greek and Latin:
-al 2, 8, 18, 20, -ar 8, -ary 18, 20 = of, relating to
-arium ii, 24, -orium 30 = place for
-ation 33 = act of
-ence 28 = action
-er ii, 1, 20 = one who, one who [observes]
-ic 20, 25, 28, 30, 31 = of, relating to
-ical 24 = of, relating to
-ify 4, 16 = to make
-ine 24 = relating to
-ion 33 = action or process
-ious 30 = having
-ist 8 = an expert in
-ism 6 = state of being
-ite 15 = fossil
-or 1 = one who
-orium 30, -arium ii, 24 = place for
-osis 12 = the act of, process
-tion 22, 24 = state of, condition

Numbers from Greek & Latin
1/1000 or thousandth = milli- 28
1/100 or hundredth = centi- 28
1/10 or tenth = deci- 28
1/2 or half = sesqui- (and a half) 27, hemi- 13
1 = uni- 12, 22, 26, 35, mono- 26
2 = bi- 8, 11, 16, 20, 26, 34, 35, bin- 16, 18, 20, di- 26
3 = tri- iii, 11, 26, 31, tri- iii, iv, 4, 6, 8, 10, 15, 26, 28, 35
4 = quad- 26, tetra- 26, 28
5 = quin- 26, penta- 26
6 = sex- 26, hex- 26, 27
7 = sept- 26, hepta- 26
8 = oct- 26, octo- 11, 21, 26, 27, 35
9 = novem- 26, ennea
10 = dec- 26, decem- 18, 20, 26, dec- 26, deca- 26
100 or hundred = cent- 2, 4, centi- 26, 28
1,000 or thousand = mill- 26, kilo- 20
1,000,000 or million = mega- 20
1,000,000,000 or billion = giga- 20

Hey, CryptoKids!

Test your Crypto skills on these hard words:

Acropolis	lithophyte
aquasaur	kalioptomegapod
autograph	mariner
chronometer	megalith
cyclometer	Pentagon
Cyclops	periodontal
dermatology	sesquicentennial
hexapod	skeletal
hydrometer	trident
lateral	trilingual